To Abbie and the Healer, who reminded me that
you can't always see what's real
L. S. W.

To Doug, Samantha, Carter, and Duffy
A. C.

First edition 2009

Library of Congress Cataloging-in-Publication Data

Sanders-Wells, Linda.
Maggie's monkeys / Linda Sanders-Wells ; illustrated by Abby Carter. – 1st ed.
p. cm.
Summary: When Maggie reports that pink monkeys have moved into the refrigerator,
her mother and father play along and accommodate the invisible visitors, much to the frustration
of Maggie's older, reality-obsessed brother.
ISBN 978-0-7636-3326-4
[1. Imagination–Fiction. 2. Brothers and sisters–Fiction. 3. Family life–Fiction.]
I. Carter, Abby, ill. II. Title.
PZ7.S19795Mag 2009
[E]–dc22 2008028711

2 4 6 8 10 9 7 5 3 1

Printed in China

This book was typeset in Cafeteria.
The illustrations were done in black colored pencil and gouache.

Candlewick Press
99 Dover Street
Somerville, Massachusetts 02144

visit us at www.candlewick.com

Maggie's monkeys

Linda Sanders-Wells

illustrated by Abby Carter

Candlewick Press

Last week, a family of pink monkeys moved into our refrigerator.

At least that's what my little sister, Maggie, said. She announced that the monkeys were in there and put a bowl of peanuts for them next to the juice pitcher.

Nobody else could see any monkeys, but that didn't seem to matter to anybody except

me.

Dad was careful not to shut the door on their tails when he took out the mayonnaise.

Mom made banana pudding and filled an extra bowl for the monkeys.

My older sister, Kate, helped Maggie dress the monkeys in invisible clothes, which she said matched their pink fur.

I didn't think we should pretend there were monkeys in our refrigerator just because Maggie said so. After all, she's practically a baby. She even still sucks her thumb when she gets scared.

When Dad and Maggie put a DO NOT DISTURB sign on the refrigerator door, I decided things had gone too far.

I pulled Dad away and reminded him, "There aren't any monkeys in there."

He just smiled and said, "Maybe they're hiding behind the olives."

When Kate helped Maggie get the brother monkey down from the ceiling fan and put him back in the refrigerator, I whispered to her, "It's too cold in there for monkeys."

Kate whispered back, "Maybe they're polar monkeys."

When Mom let Maggie's monkeys take a bubble bath with her, I waited for Mom outside the door. "Maggie's monkeys aren't real," I told her.

Mom reached out to pop a bubble that was floating by. "Sometimes," she said, "it's hard to know what's real."

Since nobody would listen to me, I tried to get used to living with Maggie's monkeys. It wasn't easy. When she invited me to a tea party, I accidentally sat in Mrs. Monkey's lap. "Watch out!" Maggie scolded.

When Mr. Monkey sat next to me in the car, I said politely, "Oo-OO-oo." He didn't answer.

"They speak *English,*" Maggie explained.

When the whole monkey family wanted me to read them a story, I picked *Please Don't Feed the Animals.* Maggie looked at me like I was crazy. "Not that one, Jack!" she whispered. "It's about the zoo."

do
not
disturb!

By the time my friends Calvin and Grady came over, I was pretty fed up with pink monkeys.

Then Grady saw Maggie mashing up bananas and berries. “What’s that for?” he asked.

“The monkeys,” Maggie answered.

Grady looked around. “Monkeys?”

“The ones in the refrigerator,” she said.

“There are monkeys in the refrigerator?” Calvin asked. He and Grady started giggling. “Are they for dessert?”

Maggie's eyes got big. "You don't eat them!" she said. "You play with them."

Calvin and Grady burst out laughing.

Grady went to the refrigerator and started to open it.

"No!" Maggie cried. "They'll get away."

They were really laughing now. "We just want to see," Grady said. He reached for the door again.

Maggie's face was red, and tears were starting down her cheeks.

"NO!" she yelled.

She jammed her thumb into her mouth and gave it a quick, worried suck.

I stepped in front of the door.

"Hey!" I said. "Can't you read? The sign says DO NOT DISTURB."

"Oh, right," Grady said. "Do not disturb the *monkeys.*"

"That's right." I didn't move. "Do NOT disturb the monkeys."

"There aren't any monkeys in your refrigerator," Calvin said.

do
not
disturb!

"Are you sure?" I asked. "Maybe they're hiding behind the olives."

"They can't be. It's too cold in there for monkeys," Grady said.

"Not these," I answered. "They're polar monkeys."

Calvin and Grady looked at each other. "You have polar monkeys in your refrigerator?" Calvin asked.

"Yep," I said, drying Maggie's face. She sniffed and looked up at me. "Pink ones."

I looked down at Maggie. She was starting to smile again. I bent and picked up something from the floor. "I think Mr. Monkey dropped his hat," I told her.

She pulled her thumb from her mouth and pointed at my hand. "That's a shoe," she said, sounding a little sorry for me.

do not dist

I shrugged, then turned back to my friends. I felt Maggie take a step closer and lean against me.

"A family of pink polar monkeys moved into our refrigerator last week," I said.

"And we're keeping them."